Copyright © 1992 by Max Velthuijs
First published in Great Britain in 1992 by Andersen Press Ltd.

Library of Congress Cataloging in Publication Data

Velthuijs, Max, 1923-Frog in winter/by Max Velthuijs.—1st U.S. ed. p. cm.
Summary: Frog's physiology does not permit him to enjoy winter,
but his friends help him to make the best of the cold weather.
[1. Frogs—Fiction.   2. Winter—Fiction.   3. Animals—Fiction.] I. Title.
PZ7.V5Fs 1993 [E]—dc20 92-20545 CIP AC
ISBN 0-688-12306-6 (TR).—ISBN 0-688-12307-4 (LE)
1 3 5 7 9 10 8 6 4 2
FIRST U.S. EDITION, 1993

Max Velthuijs
Frog in Winter

Tambourine Books · New York

When Frog got up one morning, he realized at once that something was wrong with the world. Something had changed.

He went to the window and was astonished to see that everything was completely white.

He rushed outside in confusion. There was snow
everywhere. It was slippery under his feet. Suddenly he felt
himself falling over backward, down the bank,

into the river. But the river was frozen and Frog lay on his back on the cold, hard ice. "If there's no water, I won't be able to wash," he thought, shocked.

Shivering with cold he sat on the bank. Then Duck came hurrying toward him on her skates. "Hello, Frog," she said. "Nice weather today! Are you coming skating?"

"No, I'm freezing," replied Frog.
"But skating is good for you," said Duck. "I'll teach you."

So Duck gave Frog her skates and her scarf. She pushed him and he slid quickly across the ice, but not for long. Soon, he fell.

"Aren't you enjoying yourself?" said Duck. But Frog was nearly frozen solid and his teeth were chattering.

"You've got a warm feathery coat, but I'm just a bare frog," he said.
"You're right," said Duck, "you'd better keep my scarf. Now I must be on my way."

Then Pig appeared with a basket of firewood on his back.
"Aren't you freezing Pig?" asked Frog.
"Freezing?" said Pig. "No, I'm enjoying the fresh,
healthy air. Winter is the most beautiful season."

"You have a nice layer of fat to keep you warm. But what do I have?"
"Poor Frog," thought Pig. "I wish I could help him."

One, two! One, two! Hare ran up. He was jogging in the snow.
"Hurrah!" he called joyously. "Exercise makes you healthy! Hurrah for exercise! Three cheers for exercise!"

"Why don't you join in Frog? It's great fun keeping fit."
"I'm freezing," said Frog. "You've got warm fur, but I have
nothing." Sadly, he went home.

The next day his friends invited him to have a snowball
fight. But Frog couldn't share in the fun.

"I'm freezing, I'm only a bare frog," he murmured, and miserably he stumbled home.

He sat next to the fire for the rest of the day, dreaming of spring and summer. He burned every last piece of wood.

When the fire went out he went outside to gather more logs, but he couldn't find any wood in the snow.

He walked and walked until he lost his way. Everything was white. Exhausted he lay down in the snow, a bare frog.

And there his friends found him.
"I'm freezing," whispered Frog.
"Come on," said Hare, and carefully they carried him
home and put him to bed.

Hare collected wood and lit a fire. Pig cooked a nourishing soup and Duck cheered Frog up.

In the evenings, everyone listened while Hare read wonderful stories about spring and summer. Meanwhile, Pig knitted Frog a warm pullover in two colors. Frog enjoyed the attention from his friends. Winter is wonderful when you can spend it in bed!

Then the day came when Frog was well enough to get up.
Without fur, fat, or feathers, but dressed in his new
pullover, he took his first steps in the snow.
"Well?" asked Hare curiously.
"It's good," answered Frog bravely.

So the long winter passed. But one morning when Frog
opened his eyes he noticed at once that something was
different. Bright light streamed in the window. Quickly,
he jumped out of bed and ran outside.

The world was bright green and the sun shone in the sky.
"Hurray!" he cried. "It's good to be a frog. How wonderful.
I can feel the sun's rays on my bare back."
His friends were happy to see Frog so cheerful.

"What would we do without Frog?" laughed Hare.
"I can't think," said Pig.
"No," agreed Duck, "life just wouldn't be the same
without him."